ABCs of Advent

To Carter and Cooper,
May God bless you
with peace, joy, hope
and love this season.
You are greatly loved
and been given much!

Anita Brock Bryant

Anita Brock Bryant

AuthorHouse™
1663 Liberty Drive
Bloomington, IN 47403
www.authorhouse.com
Phone: 1-800-839-8640

First published by AuthorHouse 9/30/2009

ISBN: 978-1-4490-3151-0 (sc)

Library of Congress Control Number: 2009910143

Printed in the United States of America
Bloomington, Indiana

This book is printed on acid-free paper.

authorHOUSE®

This book is dedicated to all the children who have participated in ministry with me in Waco, Texas, Louisville, Kentucky, Tuscumbia, Alabama, New Orleans, Louisiana and Young Harris, Georgia. This book is a result of our journey together to learn more and share more about the love of Jesus.

A special thank you to my children, Katherine, Matthew and Grady who supported me on this project with their opinions, their smiles, their art work, and the times of being quiet and nice to one another so that I could work. Thank you to my husband, Tim, who has supported this project even as he worked on his own PhD dissertation. I must also express thankfulness to my parents, who have guided me on this lifetime journey and have encouraged me on this particular adventure. Gracious appreciation also goes to my friend and partner in ministry, Cathy Anderson, who has kept me sane and focused, who has laughed and cried with me and who has supported me in her prayers, through her encouragement and by her forever friendship in our journey together to strive to be the hands and feet of Jesus to teach the Kingdom of God to the children of God.

A is for Angel.

Read Luke 1: 19, 24 and Luke 1: 26 – 38.

In our Christmas story there is an angel named Gabriel who visited two special women and delivered a message from God of things to come. The first visit that he made was to Zechariah and his wife Elizabeth to tell them they would have a baby. They had prayed a long time for a baby and God sent Gabriel to tell them the good news. This baby was named John and grew up to be known as "John, the Baptist." He was also Jesus' cousin.

The second visit that Gabriel made was to a young girl named Mary. He also told her that she was going to have a baby. But this baby would be God's baby and his name was to be Jesus. Having an angel visit must have been very scary for Mary. But the angel came to tell both Mary and Elizabeth something important and both of these women listened to the message that God had sent them.

We might not ever have an angel visit us. But if God used angels so long ago, perhaps God uses angels even today in new and different ways. Mary and Elizabeth were just average people, just like you, and they were chosen by God to do something very special. Did you know that you have been chosen to do something special and important too? Can you think of a special job God might want you to do today? Do you know someone who needs a word of encouragement or a hug? Can you give a special gift to someone who is hungry today? Do you have clothes that you do not wear anymore that you can donate to your neighborhood thrift store? These might not seem like special things to you. But to those who are sad, lonely, hungry or poor, these are simple things that could make a real difference in the lives of others around you. You too could be a messenger of God!

Write one thing that you can do this week to help someone.

_____

_____

_____

_____

B is for Bethlehem.

Read Luke 2: 1-4.

Bethlehem is the town where Jesus was born. At the time, Bethlehem was not a big city. It was more of a town. It was not even a really important town in the days of Jesus. It was mainly a place with a few inns, a few shops and a few shepherds who raised their sheep outside of town. But an Old Testament prophet knew that the town of Bethlehem would one day be important. The prophet was named Micah and he told the people of his day that God had said, *"Bethlehem, you are one of the smallest towns in the nation of Judah. But [I] will choose one of your people to rule the nation-- someone whose family goes back to ancient times." (Micah 5: 2, CEV)* I am sure that the people of Bethlehem waited and *waited* and **waited** for the ruler that God had promised them. It may have been so long that they may have even forgotten the promise. But then, one day, Jesus was born in Bethlehem. The smallest town in Bethlehem became a city of great importance.

Just like Bethlehem, you may feel like you are not very important or too small or young to do anything important. But something wonderful happened in the very small town of Bethlehem. Something wonderful can happen to you too. You see, you are not too young or too small to do something important for Jesus. You never know when God will use you. The people of Bethlehem did not know that their town would become a town that would be remembered for 2000 years as the birthplace of Jesus. Who knows? A small act of kindness today may turn out to be something more important than you ever thought. What did you write down yesterday as the special job you could do this week? Think back and see if you did something yesterday that helped someone. Can you find another small thing to do for someone today?

Advent Challenge: Find the book of Micah in your Bible. Then, find chapter 5, verse 2 and read it. Micah is a very small book, but it is an important book to be able to find.

C is for Candles.

Read Romans 11: 29 and Ephesians 4: 7.

During the season of Advent, we light candles to help us remember the gifts that God has given us. We celebrate with an Advent wreath that has five candles: three purple candles, one pink candle and one white candle. The candles represent special gifts from God. The gift of **Hope** is represented by the first purple candle, which is lit on the first Sunday of Advent. The gift of **Peace** is represented by the second purple candle, which is lit on the second Sunday of Advent. The gift of **Joy** is represented by the pink candle, which is lit on the third Sunday of Advent. The gift of **Love** is represented by the last purple candle, which is lit on the fourth Sunday of Advent. The white candle, located in the center of the wreath, represents the gift of Jesus. The white candle is called the *"Christ Candle"* and is lit on Christmas Eve or Christmas Day.

What wonderful gifts! Today, as you go through the activities of your day, take some time to look for something that reminds you of these gifts of Advent. Can you find something that reminds you of or gives you hope? Can you find something to help you think of peace? What brings you joy? Can you think of something that reminds you of the love of God? Most of all, can you find something that helps you to remember Jesus?

Today I found these things to remind me of God's gifts of Advent:

HOPE _____

PEACE _____

JOY _____

LOVE _____

JESUS _____

D is for Dreams.

Read Matthew 1: 18-21 and Matthew 2: 13-14.

Do you remember your dreams? Sometimes dreams can be really odd. Sometimes they can be scary. Often dreams are forgotten quickly. Did you know that the Christmas story has dreams in it? Let's take a look.

Joseph is the dreamer in our Christmas story. He actually had two dreams. Joseph had his first dream before Jesus was born. Joseph was engaged to Mary and had planned to marry her soon. But Joseph found out that Mary was pregnant and was not too sure about believing her story about the angel visiting her. Now, in those days, Joseph could have had Mary stoned to death if he didn't believe her. But he had decided that he would just not marry her at all. However, an angel appeared to Joseph in a dream. He told Joseph that Mary was telling the truth and the baby was God's baby. The angel told Joseph not to worry and to go ahead and marry Mary. The angel also told Joseph to name the baby, Jesus. So, Joseph remembered his dream, believed that God had used an angel to speak to him through his dream and did as the angel said.

The second dream that Joseph had was after Jesus was born. Again, God used Joseph's dream to tell him what he should do. An angel appeared to Joseph again in a dream and told him to take Jesus and Mary and travel to Egypt. The angel told him that King Herod wanted to kill baby Jesus. So, Joseph did as the angel instructed and traveled with Mary and Jesus to Egypt and stayed there until King Herod died.

Remembering our dreams, as Joseph did, is really hard. However, what is important to remember is not that Joseph had dreams and remembered them, but that he did what God told him to do. God talks to us in many different ways. God uses ways that we will remember. Joseph remembered dreams and that's what God used to let him know important messages. Sometimes, God uses other people to tell us a special message, like a pastor or a teacher. Sometimes God uses the Bible or hymns to teach us lessons. Sometimes, God uses dreams or even daydreams to tell us something important.

What important message do you think God wants you to hear today? Take some time today to think about, and perhaps even to dream about, what God might want you to do someday. God has something special for you to do. Will you be willing, like Joseph, to listen and follow God?

E is for Emmanuel.

Read Matthew 1: 22-23.

Did you know that Jesus is known by several names in the Bible? Emmanuel is one of those special names. Did you know that names often have meanings? Do you know what your name means? If not, take some time to ask your parents or other family members, how to find out what your name means.

My name, _____, means_____.

In Bible times, people named their children with names that had special meanings. Names were considered very important because parents wanted their children's names to reflect a special character quality. It was believed that a person's name would shape the person's thoughts and actions. Names were chosen very carefully.

Emmanuel means *"God with us."* God sent Jesus to us so that we could know more about God. Jesus is God's son. So, when Jesus was born, God was actually with us here on earth too. This was true for long ago and it is true for us even today. Jesus told us that he would be with us always, even until the end of the world. Wow!

What helps you remember that God is with you? Is it when your parents tuck you in at night? Is it when lightning and thunder crashes outside and you remember that God is there to keep you safe? God is always with us and Jesus was born so that he could tell us that important message. Even his name tells us what he wanted us to know. Jesus was important to God. God even planned that Mary and Joseph would give him the name that would shape Jesus' thoughts and actions. *God is with us. God is with you.*

Can you remember a time when you felt that God was with you?

Write it down here or draw a picture below the lines.

_____

_____

_____

_____

F is for Fragrance.

Read Matthew 2: 11.

The smells of Christmas are so wonderful: the spicy smell of cinnamon, the crisp pine smell of Christmas trees, the warm, delicious smell of cookies baking in the oven or hot chocolate in a mug with melted marshmallows. Fragrances play an important part in our Christmas celebrations. They often remind us of people and events that make Christmas so special. What fragrances of Christmas do you like best?

I like the smell of _____

It reminds me of _____

Fragrances played an important part in the first Christmas too. When the Wise Men brought gifts to Jesus, they brought gold, frankincense and myrrh. Frankincense and myrrh are two particular fragrances that held special meaning for the Wise Men and the baby Jesus. Frankincense was a kind of incense that priests would burn in the Temple to honor God. The gift of frankincense meant that the Wise Men believed that Jesus would become a priest, a minister of God. Myrrh is a fragrance that was typically used at the time of someone's death. The Wise Men believed that Jesus would need myrrh when he died.

What smells of Christmas help you to remember the birth of Jesus? We may not have frankincense and myrrh around the house, but there may be a favorite fragrance that helps you remember the meaning of Christmas. Try to smell something today that helps you to remember the birth of Jesus.

Advent Challenge: Make something fragrant today. Perhaps you could make some hot chocolate for your family tonight or help make some cookies to give to your teachers. Perhaps you could make another fragrant gift to give someone for Christmas. Be creative!

G is for Gold.

Read Matthew 2: 11 and Philippians 4: 8.

Gold is something that is usually very expensive. Not just because it is shiny and makes pretty jewelry, but because it is really hard to find. During the 1800s in the United States, there were several "Gold Rushes" is the states of Georgia, California and Colorado. People were finding gold and were getting rich! Those who heard about it thought that they could get rich quick too and they "rushed" to find gold. But gold is not so easy to find. Most gold is found deep underground. Those who rushed to get rich quickly found that they had to work extremely hard to find even a little bit of gold. They would often spend several months or even years digging tunnels through mountains and hauling out dirt to find gold. Minding for gold was also very dangerous. People would use dynamite to make holes through mountains and those tunnels would often collapse. Many were killed searching for gold. Today,

mining for gold is a little safer because we have better ways of finding it and better tools that tell miners when it is unsafe to be in a tunnel. Still, looking for and finding gold is hard and dangerous work even today.

During the time of Jesus, gold was <u>really</u> hard to find and it was so expensive that only kings and other rulers actually had any gold. The most important building with gold in it was the Temple in Jerusalem and its purpose there was to praise God. The Wise Men from the east brought baby Jesus a gift of gold. A gift of gold was only reserved for kings and for God. And do you know what? **Jesus was both.**

A gift of gold was quite special. What special gift can you think to give Jesus this Christmas? Jesus does not want or need expensive gifts from us like gold. Most of all, he wants us to love him and do our very best to be like him. Sometimes that can be as hard as finding gold.

Today, try to do your very best in whatever you do as a gift for Jesus. Remember that being perfect is not important. Talking to him, loving him and doing your best is more precious to Jesus than all the gold in the world.

H is for Herald.

Read Luke 2: 10-14.

During Advent we often sing a Christmas carol called, *"Hark! The Herald Angels Sing,"* which was written by Charles Wesley, a famous hymn writer and one of the founders of the Methodist church. We know the tune and we sing it every Christmas, but have you ever thought about what you are singing? What exactly is a *herald*, anyway? ***A herald is a person with authority who announces an important message.*** During colonial times in the United States, heralds would stand in the center of town ringing a bell and shouting an important message or the major news of the day. They did not have newspapers, television, cell phones or the internet in those days!

Now, since we are talking about the meaning of words, have you ever thought about what the first word of this carol means? **"Hark"** is an old-fashioned word meaning *"to listen."* With the exclamation mark (!), the word *"Hark"* means to *stop everything that you are doing, pay attention and <u>really</u> listen.* So, "Hark! The Herald Angels Sing" really means to ***stop everything, pay attention and listen carefully to the important angels (messengers). They have a great and wonderful message to tell you.*** So, what was that message?

There is a newborn King born

in Bethlehem who will bring us peace!

Wow! What an important message! Stop everything! Pay attention! Listen to the Herald – the Messengers with an important message to give you! The news is great! Christ the King is born!

You, too, can be a herald; a messenger with an important announcement. What important message can you tell someone today about Christmas? How does it feel when others listen to you? You do not have to shout your message in the middle of the school cafeteria, but there are other ways that you can tell others about the news of Christmas. Could you make a phone call, write an email, or maybe send a text message? Maybe you could get your message to others by showing kindness to someone today or being peaceful when others are anxious with worry.

One thing that I have learned today about Christmas is

_____

I am going to be a herald by using _____ to tell others what I've learned.

I is for Innkeeper.

Read Luke 2: 7.

You may find this amazing, but the Christmas story in the Bible does not really have an innkeeper. The Bible <u>does</u> tell us that all the inns in Bethlehem were full, so perhaps we can assume that there were innkeepers. So, today, we are going to use our imaginations to try to understand what it may have been like in Bethlehem on the night that Jesus was born.

Imagine. Everyone who was related to King David was in this little town by orders from the Roman Emperor so that he could count them all. The population of Bethlehem went from a few hundred people to thousands. The streets were full of people who had traveled long distances. Have you ever been on a long trip? Imagine how you feel when you are on a trip like that. All these people were hungry, cranky and tired from traveling. So, what did they all want when they finally got to Bethlehem? They wanted a warm place to stay and some food. This does not seem to be asking for much – on a normal night in Bethlehem. But this was no ordinary night!

So, imagine that the innkeeper tried to help as many people as he could and put as many people in his inn that could possibly fit. Imagine people not only sleeping on beds, but on the floors, on the windowsills, under and on top of tables, even in the kitchen. Imagine the noise – people who were tired and grouchy, yelling at each other to be quiet; babies crying; children saying things like, *"But I don't want to sleep with Benjamin, he always wets the pallet."* Close your eyes for a moment and image this scene. Hear the noises. See the people.

Now, imagine Joseph knocking on the door. The door opens. Joseph asks for some space. "No room!" the innkeeper shouts over the noise. He shuts the door. Joseph knocks again. "Please," he says, "anywhere will do. My wife is going to have a baby soon." The innkeeper opens the door again, looks into their faces and has compassion on them. He gives them the only space he has: a stable.

The innkeeper's job was very hard that night. But in the middle of it all, he gave what he could. He probably never knew that God's son was born in his stable that night. But he did what he could, even though he was busy and tired.

Christmas is a very busy time of year. Even so, we need to take a little time out to stop and notice those around us. Today, follow the example of our imaginary innkeeper and stop for just a moment to notice someone who may need your help. Then, find a way to help them, even if you are busy and tired and grumpy.

Today, I stopped and noticed

_____

_____

_____

I helped by

_____

_____

_____

J is for Joy.

Read Luke 2: 20.

"Joy to the World, The Lord is come!" Do you know this famous hymn of Christmas? It is sung in churches all around the world throughout the season of Advent and Christmas.

Have you ever thought about joy? What brings you joy at Christmas? Is it the thought of opening all your gifts on Christmas Day? Is it giving a surprise gift to someone special? Is it having hot chocolate after playing outside in the cold or getting to eat a warm cookie right out of the oven? Is it visiting your grandparents or seeing your cousins, aunts and uncles again for a day of fun?

Joy is an exciting thing that makes us feel warm and happy inside. But it is a special gift from God. What is even more amazing is that God gives us this gift throughout the year, not just at Christmas time. God sent Jesus to show us that joy can happen in the little moments too, like when a baby was born in a stable outside a small town a long time ago. Joy can happen when we least expect it, like an encouraging word from a teacher or a friend.

So, look for something that gives you joy. Then, share your joy with others. You may be surprised how fast joy spreads to everyone around!

This is what gave me joy today:

_____

_____

_____

K is for King.

Read Matthew 2: 1-12.

When we think about a king, we sometimes think about Jesus as King or King David or King Solomon from the Old Testament. But the king in our Christmas story, King Herod, is the "bad guy." We do not often talk about him because he is the mean person in our happy story about Jesus' birth. Still, we can learn something even from a person as mean as King Herod.

King Herod was a very selfish person that had to have his way all the time. He had to be in control of everything and everybody. He was suspicious of everyone, even his own children. No one dared to disagree with King Herod.

One day, some important travelers from the East came to see King Herod. They asked, "Have you heard that a new king has been born? Do you know where to find the new king? We want to visit him." They had traveled far to find this special king and to give him gifts. Herod was steamed! A new king was born in <u>his</u> land!? **He** was the king and **no one** was going to be king but **him**! So, Herod thought he would just trick these travelers into telling him where the new king was, so that later, he could go and kill this "new king." Then, **he** would be the **only** king again.

You see, King Herod had all he ever needed or wanted. *He was the King.* But he was so worried that someone would take all his power and all his things away from him that he became selfish and mean. He would do *anything* to keep his power and position.

Have you ever wanted something so bad you thought you would do anything to get it? During Christmas we often make lists of things we want. But have you ever made a list of things you want to give? Herod was so focused on what he wanted that he missed the reason the travelers wanted to find the new king. They wanted to *give* him gifts. Herod wanted to kill Jesus because he thought that Jesus would take away everything he had.

Christmas is not about getting things we want. If we get everything we want, we have a chance of becoming selfish like Herod. Christmas is about giving to others. The things that we have are never as important as people. So, today, make a list of gifts you want to give instead of what you want to get. Then look back at the list you made of things for which you want. Which list is longer? If your list for *"getting"* is longer than your list for *"giving,"* how can you fix it to reflect the example of the travelers in our Christmas story? Who knows? You might even notice that you do not want as much as you thought you did.

My Giving List

1. _____
2. _____
3. _____
4. _____
5. _____
6. _____
7. _____
8. _____
9. _____
10. _____

Day 12

L is for Love.

Read Matthew 5: 43-48 and I Corinthians 13: 1-8.

Do you love someone? Surely your answer would include moms and dads, grandparents, brothers, sisters, cousins, aunts, uncles, teachers, God, Jesus, friends and perhaps a few dogs, cats and birds. We love and care for all sorts of people in our lives, even our pets.

Although love is something that is easy to give to those we know and like, it is not so easy to give it to those we do not know or do not like. You may not like person who sits next to you in class that is bossy and steals your pencils. You do not really know the child on television who lives in Africa who cannot go back to his home because of a war. It is hard to really love these people.

Sometimes it is even hard for us to love ourselves. You may think your hair is too straight or too curly; or that you are too short or too tall. You may think that your teeth look funny or your feet are too big. Sometimes it is hard to love ourselves.

But God is different. God loves everyone. Even people like King Herod. God sometimes does not love the choices that we make, but God loves *who we are* because God made us. God did not think that we understood how much he really loved us, so Jesus came to tell us. Jesus loves us as God loves us and showed us a better way to love and treat others.

Sometimes it is easy to love. Sometimes it is hard to love. But we need to know that God loves everyone. God will help us love those who are hard for us to love.

Is there someone in your life that is hard for you to love? Ask God to help you learn to love that person. Pray for that person today. Perhaps, you may find that loving that person will be a little easier.

14

Dear God,

You tell us to love everyone and sometimes that is really hard. _____ is really hard to love because _____. But today, I want to try to start to love them like you do. I know I do not have to love the things they do, but help me to start by praying for _____. Let _____ know that you love him/her by my actions, my choices and my words.

Amen.

M is for Manger.

Read Luke 2: 7, 15-16.

Do you know what a manger is? A manger is a long, open container out of which animals eat. My Grandpa was a cattle farmer in West Texas when I was a child. My brother and I would often go with him to the farm to feed the cows. He would haul the hay out of the barn, put it in the truck and we would drive out together to feed the cows. He would break up the bales of hay and put it in a "v-shaped" box. This box was a manger. After we left, the cows would come and eat their hay out of the manger.

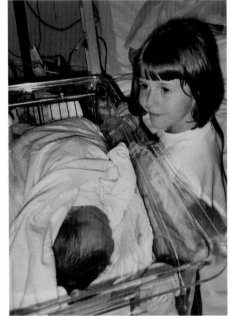

Baby Jesus, God's son, was placed in a manger after he was born. When my children were born, they were wrapped in soft blankets and slept in a nice, warm bed in a clean hospital. Jesus was not born in a hospital. He was born in a stable. His bed, the *only* thing his parents could find to lay him, was on some scratchy hay on which cows had slobbered. It was not a very nice smelling place either. Stables are pretty smelly places. It is not exactly the place where you would expect a king to be born, much less a place good enough for God's only son to be born.

But God wanted Jesus to be just like anyone else. He didn't want Jesus to be a celebrity that had to be treated special just because of who he was or where he was born. God wanted people to know that he loved those who were poor and lonely and cold and smelly. So, Jesus' first bed was a manger. Maybe it was not so bad after all. At least he had warm straw to lie on and a place out of the cold, damp air. Mary and Joseph were thankful for the stable and the manger, simple as it was.

A manger is not a fancy place, but it was good enough for God. Perhaps we think too much of fancy things. Perhaps we need to be happy with simpler toys and fewer things. Maybe we need to notice those every day, normal things we already have in our rooms.

There is a song called *"Simple Gifts"* that a religious group called "Shakers" would sing long ago. Is there a simple gift you can give this Christmas? Simple things can be more important and sometimes even more loved than things that are fancy. Can you think of something in your room that is simple, but which is important to you? Do you have an old stuffed animal that you have had since you were a baby or a book that you love to read that is worn?

What is something simple, like the manger, for which you are thankful? Be happy and thankful for the things that you have, whether they are simple or extraordinary.

I am thankful for:

_____

_____

_____

Draw a picture of something you are thankful for too!

N is for Noise.

Read Psalm 150.

Can you name some noises that you hear at Christmas time? There are the sounds of jingle bells and church bells to name a few. Christmas music can be heard all the time on the radio and at church. What other sounds can you think of that are heard at Christmas?

_____   _____

_____   _____

Have you ever thought about the noises made on the first Christmas? What do you think you would have heard that night if you were there? Use your imagination again. Close your eyes and think. Can you imagine what it would have sounded like to hear all the people in Bethlehem talking and hurrying through the streets? Can you imagine the sound of the wind, or the nighttime bugs, or maybe even dogs barking in the alleyways? Pretend you are in the stable now. What can you hear there? Can you imagine the cows mooing or the shuffling of the hay as the shepherds came to visit? Can you imagine the sound of the shepherds breathing heavily from their run to the stable? Can you imagine Mary singing softly to her baby? Then, imagine, up above the stable, perhaps if you listen closely, you can even hear the angels singing praises to the newborn king.

Listening for sounds and noises can be hard. Often we are too busy to stop and listen to the noises around us. Sometimes we are too noisy ourselves to hear anything else. There are even some children who cannot hear at all and therefore must "listen" by *feeling* the vibrations that noises make. Stop and listen today or maybe even *feel* the noises of Christmas around you. Say a prayer of thankfulness for these sounds that help us remember the first Christmas. These sounds are not only important in helping remember to listen to the noises of Christmas, but listening to these noises can help us practice listening to God, too.

Today, I heard these noises that reminded me of Christmas:

1. _____   4. _____

2. _____   5. _____

3. _____   6. _____

O is for Open.

Read Micah 6: 8.

On Christmas Day, there are many places that are closed. Restaurants, stores and gas stations are hard to find open on Christmas Day.

One Christmas Eve, my husband and I were traveling from Ohio to Texas. It was a very long trip. While we were traveling through Indiana, all of a sudden, we had a flat tire! We were stuck in the middle of nowhere, at night, and it seemed that we were the only ones traveling on that road. We had a spare tire, but the tools in the car to fix a flat tire were the ones for my dad's truck. It was cold, windy and dark and we had not seen anyone for 20 minutes. Since this was before cell phones, we did not have the ability to call someone to help us. However, we did have a CB radio in the car. We tried to call the police to come and help us. But even the police were not out on Christmas Eve on that lonely stretch of road. So, we changed the channel and hoped and prayed that someone would help us.

After a few minutes, we still had no answer to our calls for help. Then, all of a sudden, a voice on the CB said, "Is that you at mile marker 316?" Wow! Someone had found us! A big semi-truck pulled up in front of us and stopped. A man got out and walked toward us. "No one needs to be stuck out here on Christmas Eve," he said, "I'm on my way home myself. I have just five more miles." He helped us change our tire. We asked him if there would be any place that would be open on Christmas Eve to buy a tire because we had a long way to go. "There's a gas station just before you get to town," he said, "but they close at 11:00 p.m." We thanked him and wished him a "Merry Christmas" and headed toward town. The gas station was open when we got there at 10:45 p.m. We were so happy! We bought a new tire and then headed on to Texas.

That night we found out how Mary and Joseph may have felt that night in Bethlehem so long ago. We were stranded, cold, and hungry and nothing was open. But someone had compassion on us and helped us on our way.

Say a prayer today for places that stay open and for the people who work in these places when they would rather be with their own families. Pray also for those who stop and help others. Say a prayer for those who are cold and hungry and need help today. Pray that they will find someone who cares. Pray that they will find a place that is open.

P is for Peace.

Read Isaiah 9: 6-7.

During the Christmas season everyone seems to be running around, worrying about this and that, fighting the crowds at the shopping malls and bustling around trying to decorate and clean the house. It does not sound like a very peaceful time of year.

However, the first Christmas was probably just as busy. People were worried about things too. It was not a very peaceful time in their country either. Israel was under the control of the rulers in Rome and the Romans made all the rules. The people of Israel worried about what the next ruler would be like and they were often afraid of becoming slaves to the Romans.

Today, we pray for peace to come to the countries that have had long wars. Some countries are not fighting an "official" war, but there are bombs and other terrible things happening in these countries. We pray for peace in these places. But Christmas peace is not just a time when there is no fighting. Christmas peace is something more. Christmas peace is the kind of peace you have when everything around you is busy and going wild, and instead of being worried or afraid, you feel calm and quiet inside. The peace that Jesus gives us is the peace we feel on the inside, even if there is noise and war happening on the outside. Jesus does give the world peace from war and fighting, but those who want peace must also want to make changes.

Jesus gives us a special peace from worry. Are you worried about anything today? Write down the things that you are worried about or talk about them with your parents. Then pray today for Christmas peace. Give your worries to Jesus and let him give you peace on the inside. Jesus loves you and does not want you to worry.

Today I am worried about:

_____

_____

_____

_____

Dear God,

This is what I am worried about. Please help me not to worry. Please give me peace on the inside. Thank you for loving me.   Amen.

Q is for Quiet.

Read Acts 15: 12-13.

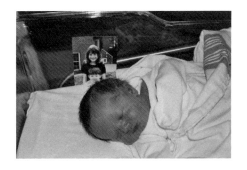

"Shhh...be very quiet." Have you ever been told to be quiet or to whisper? There are lots of places and times when it is necessary to be quiet. We have to be quiet in libraries so others can read. We have times in our church services that we need to be quiet so we do not disturb others as we worship together. If we are quiet during worship then we can listen too. We have to be quiet when babies are sleeping because they need lots of rest. We also have to be quiet to listen to another person while they are talking. It can be hard to hear someone when we are talking too.

Sometimes it is really hard to be quiet, isn't it? Sometimes we have to be quiet when what we really want to do is talk. It is hard to be quiet when we are excited too. But being quiet is important. If everyone talked and made noise all the time, we would not understand one another. Can you imagine what it might be like if *all* we did was talk and never listen? We would not be able to sleep or know what to do or where to go because we would all be talking instead of listening. Also, being quiet helps us to rest not only our bodies, but our minds too.

At this special time of year, we often sing a Christmas carol that uses the idea of "quiet." Do you know *"Silent Night?"*

"Silent night, holy night; all is calm, all is bright..."

Sing *"Silent Night"* today and think about how important being quiet is at Christmas time. Think about how important being quiet is at other times too. Think about how quiet it could have been on the night Jesus was born. Close your eyes and think about that night.

"Shhh...be very quiet."

R is for Remember.

Read Matthew 13: 34 and Joshua 4: 5-7.

Do you remember everything or do you have a hard time remembering? You have a lot to remember in a day. Sometimes you have to remember to make a lunch and then remember to take it with you to school. You have to remember what you studied for your tests at school. You must remember to brush your teeth at night and do your chores at home. Does someone help you remember those things?

What happens when you do not remember? There are consequences for not remembering things. If you forget your lunch, you have to eat what is offered at the school cafeteria. If you do not brush your teeth, you could get cavities and have to go to the dentist to get them filled. If you forget to feed your fish, it could die. If you forget to empty the trash can or the dishwasher, your mom might get mad or someone else would have to do your job and that is not fair either. Remembering things is hard, but forgetting can be a worry too.

Even God asks us to remember things. *"Remember the Sabbath day belongs to me." Exodus 20:8 (CEV)* Did you know that the word, *"remember,"* is used over 200 times in the Bible? Remembering must be very important to God.

So, how can we do better at remembering? God helps us to remember by using the stories of the Bible. What is one of your favorite Bible stories? What does it tell you about God? What does it tell you about how to treat others?

One of my favorite Bible stories is

_____

It tells me that God is

_____

It tells me how to treat others by

_____

Right now, we are remembering the Christmas story. It has so much to teach us. What have you learned from this story over the last few days? Does remembering this story help you remember things about God or how God wants us to treat others?

Stories help us remember and the Bible is full of stories. Even Jesus used stories to teach others about God. But here is the key to remembering: *you must tell or listen to the stories over and over again*. You remember the Christmas story because you have heard it told many times. You remember other stories of the Bible because you have heard them over and over again. You remember spelling words because you practice them over and over. Remembering is best done through repetition or repeating things over and over and over again. It may sound dull and boring to do things over and over again, but remembering is important. Remember – it is mentioned over 200 times in the Bible!

Make a list of things that you need to remember today. But do not forget that God loves you! It is in all his stories!

I need to remember:

1. _____

2. _____

3. _____

4. _____

5. that God loves me and cares for me.

6. that stories in the Bible are important to remember because they teach me about what God is like and how to treat others.

S is for Shepherds.

Read Luke 2: 8-20.

Shepherds were not exactly considered the most important people of society during Jesus' time. Shepherds were poor and they lived out on the fields with their sheep. This everyday camping experience meant that they did not take many baths and were probably rather smelly. Being a shepherd was rather boring too. It had its moments of excitement when a sheep would wander too far or when wolves would come close to the herd at night. But for the most part, the job itself did not offer a lot of excitement. Sadly, shepherds were generally ignored by most people so, they kept to themselves out on the field.

But God thought that they were important! Important enough to be the first ones to hear the greatest news ever! God's son was born! The angels did not go to the rulers of the nations or the priests of the Temple to tell the good news of Jesus' birth. They went to the shepherds!

Do you ever feel like no one ever pays attention to you? Do you ever feel like you are not as important as someone else? Do you ever feel ignored because you feel you are too young or too small? God has not forgotten you. God thinks you are very important.

On the most important of nights, angels were sent to the shepherds to announce the birth of Jesus. Jesus would be grow up to be a person who would never ignore them, would never forget them and would pay attention to those who felt lonely and forgotten.

The shepherds could not keep this great announcement to themselves though. They went to see the baby and then they told their story to everyone who would listen to them. And the people were amazed!

So, even if you feel forgotten and ignored, God thinks you are important, because he made you and you are his creation. And who knows? Someday God may send you an important message too! Are you listening?

T is for Travel.

Read Luke 2: 4.

Have you ever had to travel a long time in a car or a plane or a bus? No matter how long the trip, it always seems to take forever to get wherever you are going. There are things to do on trips: listen to music, play games, read books, or watch a movie if you have a portable DVD player. But traveling can be boring. Plus, you have to stay buckled in your seat and loud noises are not allowed.

Well, Mary and Joseph had to travel too. But they did not have a car, an airplane or a bus. They did not even have a bicycle. They had to walk. They traveled from the city of Nazareth to Bethlehem, which was about 70 miles. In a car, it would have taken them just a little over an hour to drive. But walking definitely took much longer. If they walked 2 miles an hour for 8 hours a day, how long would it take them to walk 70 miles? _____ (see answer on next page.) Wow! That's a long time. If you think you are tired from a *car* trip, just think how tired you would be if you had to walk to where you are going!

Some of you may be traveling a long way in a car, an airplane, a bus or maybe even a train to visit family or friends over the Christmas holidays. Some of you may not be traveling at all. But the next time you travel a long way and you are getting tired of sitting and staring at the road signs, stop and think about Mary and Joseph. Maybe, just maybe, your trip will seem to go quicker than you think. Be thankful too. If no one had invented the car or the plane or the train, you might be walking too!

Say a prayer today for all those who are traveling today. Pray that they will have a safe trip. If you know someone in particular that is traveling, pray for them too.

Dear God,

_____

_____

_____

_____

Amen.

How long would it take for Mary and Joseph to walk 70 miles? 4 days

U is for Urgent.

Read Luke 2: 15-16.

If you were given an urgent message to deliver, what would you do? Would you wait a few hours and then deliver the message? Would you wait a few days or weeks and then deliver the message? Or would you leave immediately and deliver the message? Leaving immediately would be what you want to do because *"urgent"* means that something needs attention *NOW*.

The shepherds were told to go and see the baby in Bethlehem and to look for a sign: a baby wrapped in cloths and lying in a manger. Did the shepherds wait around a day or two before looking for the baby in Bethlehem? *NO! This was important! This was urgent! They had to go look right away!*

Have you ever thought what would have happened if the angels waited a few days to tell the shepherds the good news? What if the shepherds had waited a few days to begin looking for the baby about whom they had been told? Would the shepherds have found Mary and Joseph if they had waited? Fortunately, we don't have to wonder for long about the answers to these questions. The angels <u>did</u> tell the shepherds the urgent message that Jesus was born. The shepherds went *immediately* to find the baby Jesus. Then, the shepherds told the urgent message to others – *"Jesus is born! We saw him and found him just where the angels said."*

Be glad and thankful today that the angels delivered their message to the shepherds immediately. Be glad and thankful that the shepherds went quickly to find baby Jesus. Don't wait! Tell others about Jesus' birth today! It is a story that needs to be told and remembered!

V is for Valuable.

Matthew 6: 19-21.

What is valuable to you? What is so special to you that you would never want to lose it? Some people have certain pieces of jewelry that is valuable to them, like wedding rings. Others value pictures and have scrapbooks full of pictures of family and friends. There are even people in our Christmas story that had things of value. The Wise Men brought Jesus things that were valuable: gold, frankincense, and myrrh. King Herod thought he had the most valuable things in the world.

But these things are really just *things*. If these things were lost forever, we would still have something more valuable than any of these items. We have Jesus. Jesus cannot get lost or stolen. Jesus cannot burn in a fire or get damaged in a hurricane or flood. Jesus is always with us and he is a treasure of great value. We will always have things in our lives that we treasure. But, Jesus is the only treasure in our lives that is forever. Jesus will teach us what true treasure is: ***love***. Love for <u>things</u> will not last; but our love for God and others is forever.

Remember today that you are the most valuable thing to Jesus and he loves you very much!

Draw a picture or write about something that is valuable to you. Thank God for giving you the most valuable gift of all – Jesus.

W is for Worship.

Read Psalm 63: 1-3.

Worship is something that is very important. It is something we do every week at church. But sometimes it can become just a habit. It can even become something that we do because our parents make us. We go to church, sing, give an offering, listen to a sermon and go home. However, just doing all that on Sunday morning really is not worship. Worship is something we do to show God how much we love him. Singing and giving and listening are all parts of how we worship. But worship is not just going to church. Worship is actually telling God that we love him.

The Wise Men and shepherds knew what worship was. They wanted to find Jesus so that they could worship him; to show him how much they loved him. Today, we worship this same Jesus.

Tell Jesus you love him today. Sing it in a song. Tell him in a prayer. You do not have to be in a church building to worship Jesus. You can worship him in your bedroom, on a bike ride through your neighborhood or at the dinner table with your family. Worship is something we do for God. Going to a worship service is not intended to be entertainment for us. It is to tell God that we love him and thank him. It is a time to tell God that we are sorry for the things that we have not done right and a time to help others. Worship God today, anyway and anywhere you want.

Advent Challenge: Imagine that you are in charge of planning a worship service. Write out a worship service of your own. Choose what prayers to pray. Choose the hymns or songs to sing. This is your chance to plan how you would worship and praise God. What would you include in your worship service that would be different from the worship service you usually attend? What parts would be the same? Be creative!

X is for χ (Chi).

Read Zephaniah 3: 9.

Today's lesson is a little different because it will be using both the English alphabet <u>and</u> the Greek alphabet. Even though we read our Bible in English, it was originally written in Hebrew and Greek.

In Greek, our letter for today is actually a "Ch" in English. It is called a <u>**Chi**</u>, pronounced like "Ki," but it looks like an English letter "X." When translating the Greek language into English, the letter, "χ," is exchanged for the English letters "CH" and for the words that have the hard "K" sound, like in the word, *"Christ."* The word *"Christ"* in Greek looks like this -- Χηριστοσ. In the early Greek New Testament church, people would often use the letter, "χ" to represent the whole word, *"Christ."* We do the same thing in English. The word, *"Monday,"* gets shortened to *"Mon."* or to *"M."* Can you think of other words that are shortened to just a few letters or even to one letter?

Through this season you may notice a shortened version of the word, *"Christmas,"* written as *"Xmas."* The actual word, *"Christ,"* has been shortened to one letter – the letter *"X."* It has been said that when the word *"Christmas"* is shortened to *"Xmas"* it means that Christ has been "taken out" of Christmas. But if you know the history of this word, you know that it is really just substituting the Greek letter "χ" for the letters in the name, "Christ," just as Christians did long ago. Shortening the word does not take away the meaning or significance of the word itself. The abbreviation "Rd." still means "road." The abbreviation "Fri." still means "Friday." When early Christmas saw the letter "χ," they would know its meaning and remember the stories of Christ's birth and life.

So, find something today that helps you remember the story of Christmas. It can be anything – even a letter in the alphabet – English or Greek!

Y is for Year.

Read Psalm 25: 4-6 and Hebrews 13: 8.

Think back over the events of this year. What did you do this year? What exciting adventures did you have? Did you take a memorable trip somewhere or do something special with your family? Did you have moments of sadness or of disappointment? Were there times of surprise or happiness? Did you make an important decision? Did you experience something new and different?

Every year is different. Every month is different. Every day is not the same as the day before. Looking back at the year that we have had helps to remember and think about all that we have done. It helps us to remember to be thankful. It reminds us that our days go quickly. People who have not seen you in awhile often say that you have changed or grown a lot since they saw you last. Have you noticed how you have changed this year? Have you noticed that you have learned new things or accomplished something that you could not have done a year ago?

At the end of the year and now at the end of our alphabet, take some time to see how you have changed. Reflect on what you have done. Then, dream a little. Think about some things that you would like to do next year. What will be new for you? What will be the same?

Even though our days and months and years are different, know that Jesus is the same. Our Bible tells us that Jesus is the same yesterday, today and forever. Find Hebrews 13: 8 in your Bible and read this promise for yourself. ***Jesus loves you today, he loved you yesterday and he will love you forever.*** What a great promise to take into the coming year!

I would like to do these three things next year:

1. _____

2. _____

3. _____

Z is for Zion.

Read Psalm 146.

Today's word contains the last letter of the alphabet to end our Advent preparations for Christmas. It is not a word that you would usually hear, except in your church. There is a hymn that is sung in many churches called, *"We're Marching to Zion"* and it is sung in churches all over the world.

Zion is also a word found in the Bible. It was the name of a special mountain named ***Mount Zion*** on which King David built his capital city.   It was considered a holy and special place. However, in many places in the Bible where Zion is mentioned, it is not talking about the actual mountain of Zion, but rather it is talking about the holy and special place that we call "heaven." In fact, the word "Zion" is mentioned 130 times in the Bible and only a few of these are about Mount Zion.

So, what does Zion have to do with our Christmas story? You see, Jesus left his place in heaven to come be with us here on earth to show God's love to all people. It has been a continuing theme throughout the Bible. God has been trying from the time of Creation to show us how much he loves us. The Christmas story is a continuation of that design and purpose. The greatest thing about this is that this story never ends. Zion is where Jesus went to prepare a place for us. Zion is the place where love lives forever. It is the perfect ending to our days of preparation. God shared his love for us through his son, Jesus, who came as a baby to world full of people that needed to hear again that God loved them. The message is the same today: God loves you and waits for you in heaven, in Zion, so that he can love us and we can love him – forever.

The Christmas story is not just for Christmas. It is a place to begin to really understand the love of God, no matter what season of the year it is. Retelling the story over and over again, not only helps us to remember this wonderful story, but helps us learn new lessons of hope, of peace, of love and of joy to carry with us throughout our lifetime, so that one day, we will celebrate together with Jesus in Zion.

LaVergne, TN USA
15 October 2009
160905LV00002B